Words on a Faded T-Shirt

NORMAN SILVER

faber and faber
LONDON · BOSTON

For Jack and Belle

First published in 1991
by Faber and Faber Limited
3 Queen Square London WC1N 3AU

Photoset by Wilmaset Birkenhead Wirral
Printed in England by Clays Ltd, St Ives plc

ISBN 0−571−16127−8

Contents

Two Boyfriends

One sends me Turkish delights
inscribed with love lyrics
and wrapped in pink ribbons.

The other rides a Kawasaki.

One has dreams with subtitles
and investigates psychic phenomena
with litmus paper and tweezers.

The other rides a Kawasaki.

One has telephoto eyes
for capturing the folk-dances of water
and the conversations of clouds.

The other rides a Kawasaki.

One eats only free-range fruit
and cries when he sees children
partying at McDonald's.

The other rides a Kawasaki.

One talks to God in his spare time
and knits him jumpers
and warm woolly hats.

The other rides a Kawasaki.

One believes that our two names
are written somewhere on a golden scroll
and that sex is meaningful.

The other rides a Kawasaki.

Oh Dear

There's a hole in the ozone, dear Liza, dear Liza.
A hole in the ozone, dear Liza, a hole.

   Ozone, what can the matter be?
Why are they talking about a catastrophe?
It's just a hole in our planet's anatomy.
   Nobody knew it was there.

   Ozone, what can the matter be?
Is there a puncture in your circularity?
Can we repair it with band-aid and charity?
   Nobody knew it was there.

   Ozone, what can the matter be?
Is your wound hidden by blankets of secrecy?
Have you been injured by doses of CFC?
   Nobody knew it was there.

   Ozone, what can the matter be?
The profits are high at our chemical factory.
All our precautions are quite satisfactory.
   Nobody knew it was there.

   Ozone, what can the matter be?
Surely pollution is something that had to be.
Blame all the others, I know that it wasn't me.
   Nobody knew it was there.

Ozone, what can the matter be?
Why are they talking about a catastrophe?
It's just a hole in our planet's anatomy.
    Nobody knew it was there.

Well fix it, dear Henry, dear Henry, dear Henry.
Well fix it, dear Henry, dear Henry, fix it.

Postcard

The ocean blows its snotty nose
on the cold beach, observed
by gossipy old geraniums

nicely tucked up in their beds.
Only a single tourist,
beguiled by the oily rainbows

flashing neon in the waves,
goes for a lucky dip
and finds plastic treasures

to place upon his mantelpiece.
Presently a lady, a lady
comes walking, walking her dog.

Their two fine snouts
sniff the early evening breeze.
There's a lot of shit about.

The leprous grins of bankrupt
comedians peel from the pavilion:
an act that is hard to follow.

Above the waterfall, piddling
its pea-green into the pond
where the puffy goldfish float,

in the shelter where the ancients
used to look out to sea, thinking
about tomorrow and tomorrow,

a boy of fifteen sea-side years
bags his head with polythene.
He is about to go deep-sea diving.

Good Sport

The afternoon was dressed in white socks and zero
was politely called love to disguise the fact that Dad
always beat the hell out of me. He was not that good
at tennis; just that I was worse, so he always won.

At tea-break, I wandered off, leaving Dad chatting up
the birds that strutted teasingly between chairlegs.
The stream was swollen, festering a formaldehyde froth.
I sat a moment on a stone seat in a holographic cinema

like a nature lover, watching the tumbling formations
plunge from a level above. The cream on the scones
Dad had with tea was off, he told me some time later.
I climbed up through swirling images of water and rock

to the pool I had swum in as a child. Now a dead cow
lay in it, its body bloated like a pumped rubber glove,
eyes and nose submerged in slime and weed pastures,
neck sandwiched between boulders, with two tired feet

conducting the current. My growing arms will soon have
more strength than his, my Dad says, and then I'll win,
occasionally. But that afternoon I lost more lovegames
and white socks were forever stained the colour of cow.

Word of God

The original
nameless
unutterable
all-encompassing
neverending
pre-existing
majestic
omnipotent
everpresent
indefinable
inconceivable
self-perpetuating
effulgent
awe-inspiring
miraculous
spontaneous
polyunsaturated
(just checking to see if you're awake)
magnificent
sovereign
superconscious
immutable
unquenchable
word:
WOW.

The Pigeon

My father
with a tormented suitcase
stood at our front door
waiting for the train

that would take him
to a new house, a new wife,
a new family.
My mother

with a drowned handkerchief
lay face down on her bed
waving goodbye
to marriage.

I sat
in an attic room
bustling with departures
and people hugging each other

through jolting windows.
A solitary pigeon
perched on a high ledge
as the train pulled out.

Drinking Diary

Monday, Monday,
numberoneday.
Go get pissed –
it's weekbegunday.

Tuesday, Tuesday,
nothingtoloseday.
Stay at home –
it's beerandboozeday.

Wednesday, Wednesday,
roundthebendsday.
Join the mob –
it's pukingfriendsday.

Thursday, Thursday,
visionblursday.
Hold your tongue –
it's slipsandslursday.

Friday, Friday,
gettinghighday.
Have a snort –
it's doordieday.

Saturday, Saturday,
bloodandspatterday.
Pick a fight –
it's brawlandbatterday.

Sunday, Sunday,
hadourfunday.
Drive home drunk –
it's hitandrunday.

We Don't Want It Grey

Graffiti on the wall, graffiti on
the train, graffiti on the city street,
graffiti on your brain. Write on! There's nowhere sacred, it's a technicolour show.
Write on whatever's ugly, let the con-
crete glow. Paint your words with music, beat

your techno-pop, electro-funk your ma-
ma, rap the world: hip-hop. Across the earth
one nation, dancing through the town, and chant-
ing songs and poetry, with words you can't
put down. The brothers and the sisters, the family of man, it's gonna be the birth-

time of the spraying-can. Graffiti on
the arms, graffiti on the face of Babylon!

Dungeons & Dragons

The average game duration of this mega-fantastic quest
is three score and ten years, though several cases have
now been authenticated of people continuing to play D&D
long after brain-death. The basic idea is to pretend

you're someone else, somewhere else, doing something else.
That is called 'role-play' and is lots of fun. Usually
adventures are brimful of charm: death-rays, meteor swarms,
paralysis spells, petrification, fireballs and other items

from your mum's sewing box. If you have an aunt or uncle
who's a golem or a hippogriff, just observe them and learn.
If your dad's a doppelganger, lesser efreeti or devil swine,
consider yourself fortunate as you are likely to inherit

polymorphic abilities. This game develops personality
and after playing it for only a few weeks you will notice
improvements in your charisma, dexterity and constitution.
It is also believed to affect your wisdom and intelligence

so concerned teachers should be well-pleased. You should
never make public the fact that you continue playing D&D
during school lessons. No teachers – be they halflings,
clerics, elves or magic-users – will ever drop disguise

during school hours, though sometimes they cannot resist
making Attack Rolls with a twenty-sided piece of homework.

Bibble

In the beginning was the void –
and everything avoided it.

Then God created Heaven and Earth
and upon the Earth He placed Ipswich
and in it Tower Ramparts Shopping Centre.
And seeing that it was good
He took an escalator to the top level
and ordered a decaffeinated coffee.

And that which was, was –
and that which wasn't, didn't complain.

And on the seventh day God rested –
but on Monday he was back at work.

And Lo! it came to pass
that 'Lo!' became a popular expression
among Bibble writers.

In the beginning was the word
and from that word were many words begotten
and without them how would we play Scrabble?

And God said, Let there be light:
and there was light.
And God saw the light, that it was good:
and God divided the light from the darkness.
And God called the light Day,
and the darkness He called Night.
Good Day.
Good Night.

And God made the firmament,
and divided the waters which were under the firmament
from the waters which were above the firmament:
and it was so.
And realizing that there was a word left out after 'so',
He added the word 'zazzy'.
And it was so zazzy.

And God called the firmament Heaven.
And the ornament He called an Executive Toy.
And the parliament he called Westminster.
And the name He bestowed upon the tournament
was Olympics.
And He called the predicament Life.

And God said, Let us make man in our image.
But the mirror He used was bequirked
and man came out a spitting image.

Male and female created He them.
And God blessed them, and God said unto them,
Be fruitful and multiply —
and when He saw how much they multiplied
He gave them all pocket calculators.

Be fruitful and multiply
and replenish the earth
and subdue it.
And when He saw how fond they were of subduing it
and that the subduing had become an obsession,
and the obsession had become an addiction,
He said, I didn't say throttle it.

And the Lord God planted a garden
eastward in Eden;
and there He put the man
whom He had formed.
And He called the man James Dean
to star in it.

And the Lord God said, It is not good
that the man should be alone;
I will make him an help meet for him.
And the home help He called a Wife.

And whatsoever Adam called every living creature,
that was the name thereof.
And after a day of giving out good English names
like dog, cat, cow and goat,
Adam's tongue grew exceedingly out of control
and he gave names like
orang-outang, aardvark, kinkajou and dziggetai.

And they were both naked,
the man and his wife,
and because there were no men of morals
to spy upon them,
they were not ashamed.

Now the serpent was more subtle
than any beast of the field
which the Lord God had made,
and he coined a packet
by trading in sins
(mainly 501 originals).

And he persuaded the woman
that the tree of knowledge was good for food,
so she took of the fruit thereof,
and did eat,
and gave also unto her husband with her;
and he did eat.
And they both got a very bad upset
which was visited on them
and their children's children,
and even unto this day
visiting children can be upsetting.

And the eyes of them both were opened,
and they knew that they were naked;
and they sewed fig leaves together,
and made themselves aprons.
Which aprons were seized upon by designers
and a heavy price-tag put upon them.

And Adam knew his wife;
which was a good thing
as to not know your wife
can cause you to frequently say,
Who is this woman?
which could be embarrassing
in front of friends and relations.

And Adam knew his wife;
and she conceived,
which goes to show that it's who you know
not what you know
that gets results.

And Adam knew his wife.
And she bare Cain.
And she again bare his brother Abel.
And being so bare
she got a bit chilly.

And it came to pass that Cain rose up
against his brother and slew him.
and much slewing has there been ever since
so that it is not safe to walk anywhere
without being armed against one's brothers.

And the Lord said unto Cain,
Where is Abel thy brother?
And he said, I know not:
Am I my brother's keeper?
I am not even in his team.

Microscope

He bows his head as if at prayer:
but only one tight eye is closed
to the secular world; the other

is open – inquiring and curious.
It focuses on the great Circle
of Being where the forces of dark

and light perform their vital dance.
Magnified five hundred times,
his consciousness roams each slice

of life, moving unseen among
the mammoths of the underworld.
Here, beasts greater than a camel

pass through the eye of a needle,
feeding on flowers of crystallized
sugar or cornflakes of dead skin.

Here, in the realm of time forgotten,
name forgotten, identity forgotten,
the seeing eye is one with the seen.

Here, in the glow of a gnat's wing,
in a poppyseed honeycombed all over,
amid a forest of monolithic hairs,

ordinariness has been transmuted –
and a bored schoolboy rediscovers
the Buddha-nature of all things.

Leather Jacket

Heavy leather –
    patched and ripped.
Well-loved object,
    studded and zipped.

Hell and angels –
    been through it all.
Knifed and hacked,
    up against the wall.

Easy rider –
    travel with speed.
The world's in my pocket,
    everything I need.

Restless spirit –
    can't be owned.
Dumped and nicked,
    traded and loaned.

Genuine one-off –
    tattoos on my back.
Paint faded and flaked,
    but it's a zodiac.

Bruised and bloodied –
    stained with grease.
Caught and hooked
    by the police.

Leather jacket –
      know what I mean?
Don't expect
      that I keep clean!

Apron

Mother's apron
is stained with love;
how cleverly it covers
her passions.

The kitchen is wholly hers;
there she may tend
the dishwasher,
perform ablutions,

and minister
to the tumble dryer
or washing machine.
No one hears her curse.

Her many pots steam
and boil and hiss;
she is the lady
of potatoes and shallots.

In the smoky glass
of her dark oven
she sees shadows
of the passing world.

Her timer plings
for each hair turned grey,
for each day casseroled
in its own drippings.

Can she disown the memory
of a jewelled man
who called for dinner –
the one who hummed

as he untied the strings
behind her back
and pressed his hand
against her nakedness?

How can she deny
that the ovenglass
ominously cracked
from side to side

when she turned to him?
Didn't she cry
when he rode off,
leaving her here

to honour and serve
her dutiful god of love,
wearing an apron
and oven gloves?

Now each day
she prepares her offering;
turns down the heat
and gently simmers.

Long Jump

Concentrate,
ease into the measured run,
accelerate,
hit the springboard,
don't overstep,
lift off,
stretch legs and arms,
go for height,
as well as length,
fly . . .
the sandpit below,
the spectators,
the grandstand,
the city,
the clouds,
the blue beyond . . .

I think I'm ready to jump now.

Voyager

Dr K envisioned his own life
as a Mandelbrot function adrift
in a universe of immense possibility.

He pondered his geography
with its awesome fractal beauty,
complex and infinitely explorable.

Each granule of consciousness
pulsed rawly with kaleidoscopic
quantums of energy. By a sequence

of transformations, a granule
could be exploded into a galaxy
of previously unexplored terrains.

Dr K's reflexive mathematics
enabled excursions of discovery
to planetworlds as yet unimagined,

where mountain-peaks of light
shimmered above oceans of sound.
His graphic journal is now legendary,

with its dazzling photographs
and account of the final voyage:
how he ventured beyond the realms

of experience to the ultimate
configurations of his life-form.
But many believe he fictionalized

his endeavours, that, in fact,
he fell victim to hallucination
in an outcrop of a far-off galaxy.

Possible Careers

When I grow up I'd like to be

a surgeon performing surgery
a potter creating pottery
an archer practising archery
a sorcerer exercising sorcery
a forger pursuing forgery
a butcher perpetrating butchery
a robber attempting robbery
a cook perfecting cookery

but

I think I'll probably be
an adult . . .

Saturday Shopping

Attired in torn cloaks, goths mourn the ordinariness
of the late twentieth century: ten black bottles

sitting on the wall watching the living dead rise
from carparks. Standing by his open instrument-case,

a violinist plays a concerto like Botticelli's Venus.
Judy assaults a policeman: her baby is a dead ragdoll

doubled over Mr Punch's neglecting shoulder.
The shopping precinct church has broken windows:

a priest scrubs the word 'VAMPIRE' off his cassock.
In department stores, concepts with expensive tags

hang on racks. Violet neonlit escalators shunt
passengers up and down paradise: background music

chants its praise of purchasing on personal account.
Luminous salesgirls circulate to solicit clients,

guarantees of glamour oozing from their wares.
In cubicles behind temple walls, customers try on

new lives: mirrored clone-peacocks pose and strut
through topiaried mazes of the future. Offerings

to the great god are stashed in tills by sleek males
with pouting nostrils. While a silverhaired gent

escapes wearing two three-piece suits, security men
halfnelson a cheap embezzler behind the can-can rows

of lingerie. The manager plans a cardiac arrest.
At closing, well-heeled plastic bags drag humans

through revolving doors, haul them back to napping
cars which spiral down exit ramps like bathwater.

The city disgorges its guests. Only Count Dracula
shivers in moonlight by the churchwall and bites

a girl's neck as she sniffs from praying hands.

Gammy

This new kid has a gammy leg:
    he was born with it I think.
Wherever he goes he has to drag it along
    like a pathetic friend
    that nobody wants to know.

I like Chris, don't get me wrong.
    But I don't like his leg.
It gives me the creeps seeing it so thin
    and withered like a starving kid.
    But his other leg's strong.

I know, because he scores goals
    with it: it's got muscle.
But when he runs after a ball it's awful
    to see his uneven gallop.
    I wish they could fix him.

One day I tease him in class.
    I don't know why, I just do.
I call him a cripple and knock him over –
    hurt him until he cries.
    I make him crawl on the floor.

None of the other kids stop me.
    Too busy laughing they are.
Chris looks up at me and says something
    that hurts more than teasing.
    He says I have a gammy brain.

He says he can see it all withered.
Was I born like that? he asks.
It must be awful to be so badly crippled,
    like having a pathetic friend
    that nobody wants to know.

He says he likes me all right,
    it's just the crippled brain
I drag around that gives him the creeps.
    He says why don't the doctors
    operate on me or do something?

It's funny but now Chris
    and me are getting on OK.
I don't notice his leg callipers anymore,
    I mean I do, but they don't
    bother me like they used to.

He's into all sorts of things
    Chris is, like arm wrestling.
We're about equal, except if he cheats.
    But sometimes if I nark him
    he still calls me gammy.

Jazzy-Snazzy and Honey-Bunny

Here come fresh
curly-pearly-twirly-whirly-hurly-burly-Shirley-girlie.
She hotfire and steamy-gleamy,
make boyhead go creamy-dreamy.

What fool this
hunky-chunky-spunky-monkey-flunky-punky-funky-junkie!
He original murky-jerky,
how I roast this quirky-turkey?

Delicious
rooty-sooty-fluty-cutie-snooty-tutti-frutti-beauty.
Syrup smooth she inky-dinky,
twisty lemon slinky-kinky.

Why he look
stubby-chubby-pubby-grubby-clubby-tubby-rubby-dubby?
Fashion boy dress randy-dandy,
inside he empty andy-pandy.

For sure you
jolly-lolly-folly-dolly-holly-golly-polly-molly!
Pleasure mix we sticky-quickie,
ride goodstyle with tricky-dicky!

Me know you
scruffy-chuffy-huffy-puffy-gruffy-snuffy-roughie-toughie!
Meat and muscle scrawny-brawny,
Billy goat grow horny-corny.

Cheap talk you
saggy-slaggy-braggy-naggy-faggy-draggy-shaggy-baggy!
Why nogood girl so boozy-choosy?
Your reputation woozy-floozy.

You one big
flappy-yappy-sappy-pappy-crappy-rappy-zappy-chappie!
Blubber loudmouth manky-swanky,
pocket up your hanky-panky!

Surfing

Follow the sun: wait until
it reaches Malibu, Hawaii
or the Australian Gold Coast.
Relish a midnight barbecue
on the beach with moonlight
bouncing off tanned shoulders
into the eyes of an admirer.
Next morning place your board
on the crest of a wave the size
of Tibet. Let your consciousness
merge with the force of the sea.
Let your hair become sea-froth.
Let your body balance between
power and glory. Let your voice
be the thunder of unfurling
breakers on the infinite sand.
Let your joy be a single star
in a galaxy of liquid spirals.
Let your heart be an embryo
in the water-womb that coils
around you. Then, sea-walker,
emerge from the ocean like
an apostle from the depths
of time and have a Coke.

Girlie

Those are her chalk pavement-dragons
persistently blowing their faded fire.
The mindless ones tread over them now.

That is her penny-whistle and her cap,
still with a fountainful of coppers.
If I listen, will I hear her tunes?

That is the doorstep where she sat,
never entering and never exiting.
I always told her she'd get nowhere.

There are her shoes that never trudged
any place but the dark and back alley.
They have worn out with marking time.

That is her bag: it should be filled
with books, but they have truanted.
Now it is pregnant with jumble clothes.

That is the mirror she made up with.
In the right light you can see images
of her blackened lips and fingernails.

There is her tissue-wrapped treasure
of tablets: can they be painkillers?
My little girlie was never in pain.

And there she is with her frozen eyes.
I've never seen her this far gone,
pretending she doesn't know her mum.

Macho

She's gonna love it:
   girls do.
It's the beerbreath smell
that gets them wild.
Designer vomit
on a shirt,
glazed eyes,
staggering to the loo –
it's all crucial
to me image.

She's gonna love it:
   girls do.
The inarticulate grunt,
the lurching swagger,
a bit of violence,
blood and spew.
Riding pillion
on me Honda
as I race drunkenly
through the night,
she's gonna hug me
beerbloated belly.

She's gonna love it:
  girls do.
As I kiss her
and probe her mouth
with me bilious tongue,
she's gonna get hot.
She's gonna ask for more.
So I'll drink
until the beer leaks
from me jeans,
and we'll screw
till I pass out.

She's gonna love it:
  girls do.

Love Affair

I'm in love with a bloke
who sews designer labels on pigeons
    and feeds them coke.

He takes me to performances
of the stock exchange and applauds
    when the market dances.

Sometimes he says he's god
and puts his signature on all things
    in bright luminous red.

He drives a luxury bus.
On its sides are huge advertisements
    for Eternal Happiness,

an effective new deodorant
which he manufactures from plutonium
    on a government grant.

He plays hymns on a harp
strung with human hair and his trumpet
    is the thighbone of a bishop.

He has taught me mysteries:
how to remove a turtle from its shell
    and replace it with batteries,

how to survive Antarctica
in a centrally heated house with sauna,
    how to make a replica

human child from chromosomes.
He sings me catchy advertising jingles
      when he holds me in his arms

      and tells me love backwards
is the first four letters of evolution.
      He is consummate with words.

Last Supper

A grandfather begins with a grace
of introductions: may I introduce
so and so from such and such a place.

Gavin sits at table between an aunt
who has been laid by a busdriver
and an accurately combed accountant.

He cannot discern his girlfriend:
two buzzing males circle her face.
She flicks them off with her hand

but they persist. Her father smiles:
he already thinks of a brideprice.
Her mother serves soup and hot rolls.

Gavin patches his battered denims
with a white table napkin: his boots
rub shoulders with high-heeled madams.

Devout gentlemen talk of profits
and flotations and market trends.
Her mother serves salmon fillets.

The most dainty of the females
spills the bloody bottle of claret
when conversation turns to betrayals.

The well-laid aunt leans over Gavin.
'Be a darling and pass the butter.'
Her open blouse preaches a sermon

as she plants a kiss on his cheek
then bites her false fingernails.
Gavin's girlfriend is telepathic:

as her mother serves pickled tongue
she feels the nausea strangling him.
His eyes roll upward to the ceiling

where two glittering carousels spin;
his gullet is choked with potatoes,
and his heaving lungs gasp for oxygen.

He fights for life in the bathroom,
sucking in water and remembering
a similar trial in his mother's womb.

After the meal, the guests recline
in creamy puddings, drinking coffee
from Kenya. Gavin tries to explain

words on his faded T-shirt to a doctor
whose bleeper sounds like a churchbell
yet cannot be heard because of liquor.

As her mother serves the sacraments
Gavin's girlfriend makes her getaway.
They leave without after dinner mints.

The Den

For seven days they dug the hole
they would bury themselves in
from the world. They used shovels
and wheelbarrows and fingernails
to haul out earth and stack it

by the kitchen window. Corrugated
iron covered the gap and gravelly
earth was smoothed back with only
a gutter airhole to give away
the game. The burrow entrance

was concealed by knotted branches
and guarded, the password known
only to four. Below ground there
were shelves on which obsessions
were arrayed like bottled spices

in the mother's kitchen. As she
cooked, her broad eyes overlooked
the explorations in the clubhouse,
smells and sounds seeping through
the blowhole. Their youth ended

when the roof collapsed and four
bog creatures, half-suffocated
by secrecy, and scooping sods
of earth from their breathing
passages, clawed their way out.

Maths Problems

Using only a pair of compasses,
find the exact midpoint
of the universe.

Using Euclid,
prove that the shortest distance
between two points
is not the B1070.

Using decimals,
show that 10/11 of the population
find the government
a recurring problem.

Using only a cheap calculator,
determine the truth
of the proposition
that the universe was made in Japan.

Using Pythagoras,
prove that a politician
who is hypnotized
is equal to the sum
of any two politicians
on the opposite sides.

Using a word processor,
describe a circle of radius 20 cms
in not more than fifty words.
Do not go off at a tangent.

Using mental arithmetic,
  add up an idea,
        a dream,
         a desire,
      a memory,
    and a *déjà vu*.

Using number theory,
prove that oneness
is not irrational
but just a case of being lonely.

Using Venn diagrams,
prove that death is not an empty set
but merely the intersection
of two vastly different dodecahedrons.

Using common sense,
prove that the manyness
of the elements of a set
is best represented by a cardinal number,
whereas their common interests
are best represented by a vicar.

Using algebra,
solve the equation $x + 42y = 13z$
    where x = a prime minister,
            y = growth economics
        and z = a nightmare.

Using networks,
prove that England is traversable,
provided you avoid
the Ipswich/Liverpool Street line.

Using trigonometry,
explain why the angle
taken by national newspapers
is always more than 90 degrees.
Is it because they can't help being obtuse?

Using statistics,
demonstrate that the probability
of improving the universe
is inversely proportional to the number
of people waiting to be re-housed.
Show that the standard deviation
from such meanness is frustration.

Using logarithms,
calculate the value
(correct to four decimal places)
of a piece of advice.

Using graphs,
plot the curve of time.
Check whether it ever passes through
the same point more than once
or whether it ever returns
or whether it ever returns
to repeat itself.
Mark your own existence on the curve
with an X.

Using vectors,
show that a person
with both magnitude and velocity
is liable to suffer from stress.

Using pi in the sky,
show that 22 out of 7 people
who expressed a preference
chose Whiskas in favour
of a meal out in Ipswich.

Using calculus,
prove that it is impossible
to differentiate a man and his wealth
and equally impossible
to integrate his words and his deeds.

Using factorization, find:
 i) the Lowest Common Denominator between
            a football hooligan,
                a politician,
            and a limbo dancer.
 ii) the Highest Common Factor between
            a mountaineer,
                a junkie,
            and a pope.

Using a programming language,
write an algorithm
which allows the computer
to overcome its fear
of being a circuit
of electronic impulses
in an enclosed space.

Using any theorems you like,
prove that the distance
between yourself and the infinite
is proportional to where you're at.

Rite of Passage

For twenty-four days
he was permitted
to imbibe only ale
and ingest only chips.

The women of the tribe
were locked indoors.
He was adorned in boots
and lace-up jeans:

his head was scalped
at the barber's.
The gang clubbed together
to buy a cudgel

and let him join
the night excursions.
He was revealed
the grace of the crowbar,

the passion of mugging,
the ecstasy of loot.
For three days and nights
the sacred drug

was administered
through a punctured vein:
he experienced
the rush of existence.

The nation's mark
was tattooed on his arms,
the mark of the eagle
on his bare back.

He was instructed
in the subtlety of glass,
the dynamics of brick
and potency of petrol.

Exposed to the ridicule
of the courts,
he endured the brutalism
of the shared cell.

His emergence into manhood
was celebrated
in a condemned house
with allnight dancing,

allnight drinking
and a girl called Juicy,
who was sacrificed
to jealous gods.

Iron Rule

She runs her life like an empire:
with governors for her many children.
Her mansion has dark, secret rooms
where the handicapped and deformed
are trussed inside their limitations.
She cannot endure the sight of blood

so killings are brief trivialities
and menstruation is declared illegal.
She inaugurates complex chastisements
for the unruly elements of her soul
and calculates emotions on a scale
of non-productive to highly profitable.

She dismisses creativity as a slave
caught stealing from private orchards
or eloping with a virgin daughter.
She has the hands of gypsy violinists
surgically removed in baths of acid.
Poverty is obscene and not heard.

Those who indulge in it are traitors
to her state of happiness and banished
to ghettos where the minorities group.
Nappies are white and never soiled:
babies who disobey are tourniquet'd
and plugged with moral arguments.

She brooks no backchat: enveloped
by silent politeness and adulation,
she cultivates pride like an orchid.
When her husband suffers a *grand mal*,
she regards his unconsciousness
as a lack of affection, a rebellion

against marriage, a weakness of spirit.
She spreads the word that they never
were married: the man was an impostor.
She regards her own brain functioning
as an achievement, an accomplishment
at the expense of other life forms.

A certificate in her bedroom, alongside
faded photographs of her predecessors,
testifies to the fact that she excels
at survival of the fittest: she sees
proficient management as her ultimate
weapon in the fight against death.

Quarrel

On Sunday morning
the roses are reverent:
they congregate
in long, neat rows
and worship, worship,

while the newspaper lies
open on the path slabs,
exposing its flab
of naked passions.

My mother tended
those roses:
it is her orthodoxy
spread across the lawn
and those are her
devout borders.

From the stump pulpit
the robin asks
whether the opposite
of faithful
is faithless
or unfaithful.

Ms Quinney
from number 78
waves to me:
she's into women's lib
and her garden
is an orgy of thorn
and thistle.

My window is open:
I can smell the breath
of my mother's god
wafting between
prim conifers.

The walls of my bedroom
are so thin I can see
my stepdad snoring.
My mother rattles off
him number 3,
drums his back
with her fists
but he won't wake:
his Mercedes
rests on the seventh day.

Eclipse of the Sun

I say the sun is a ball of hot gas
at the centre of the solar system.

> You say it is the sky-god
> in the centre of your life.

I say the sun is largely composed
of the elements hydrogen and helium.

> You say its sacred substance
> is fire which breathes life.

I say the sun is 150 million
kilometres distant from the earth.

> You say it is where it is,
> the heart of all things.

I say the sun burns at 6 thousand
degrees centigrade on its surface
and over 10 million at its centre.

> You say kneel before it:
> to stare directly at a god
> will burn out your eyes.

I say the sun's gravitational field
is 28 times greater than the earth's.

You say the sun's power
enables you to walk upright
through your earth journey.

I say the sun emits light, X-rays,
radio waves, gamma and cosmic rays.

You say it wakens the earth
and enlightens the spirit.

I say the sun has a corona from which
electrically charged particles stream
into space forming vast solar winds
which affect the earth's weather.

You say the sun's bright halo
surrounds a god of great mercy
and from it stream all gifts.

I say the sun has spots and flares,
which vary both in size and number
if observed over a period of years.

You say your sky-god's face
expresses a great many moods.

I say the sun has supplied the earth
with light and heat energy for about
5 thousand million years and will
continue doing this for at least
another 5 thousand million years.

You say your shining is a brief
spark of the sun's eternity.

I say the sun is getting hotter:
in 5 thousand million years' time
it will become a giant star and life
on earth will probably be destroyed.

You say life on this earth
is a fragile thing: if it is
here tomorrow you will kneel
and thank the sky-god.

I say the sun has addled your brain
and therefore I must blindfold you.

You say the sun has let you
see your truth and it also
has let me see my truth.

I say that I must tie you to a pole
so you may denounce your beliefs.

You say that though the gun
may send fire to your head,
it cannot kill the sky-god.

I say the sun is a ball of hot gas
at the centre of the solar system.

You say nothing.

Jolly Roger

Our house is ship-shaped with an upstairs deck
for quoits and fraternizing. The flag that flies
on the mast is my tipsy Uncle Roger. My family
sails the suburbs, pirating the neighbours,
stealing their domesticity. The captain's bridge
is a room beneath the stairs with a parchment map
pinned to a dark wall. Behind the X is a vault
where he hides the day's profits. At night
he wears his nautical cap and takes his bearing
by constellations. The ship's cook knows
her galley-place. She stews enormous potfuls
of sweaty delights for storm-tossed sailors
and harbours under their exotic illusions.
I am the stowaway. Chin-deep in booty, I hear
anguished groans in the ship's belly and endure
circular visions of sea and sky. When the ship
is becalmed, the captain orders revelries:
girls are smuggled aboard and filled with rum.
From my sack I've seen Uncle, with hookhand,
woodenleg and patcheye, jig with a maiden
then throw her to the sharks. Soon I'll have
enough body hair to join the crew. I'll weigh
anchor tattoos and sing shanties in the lavatory.

The Tie

He appeared at her front door wearing
a black suit and a speckled pink tie.
In her mother's spectacled eyes he was
a convex liquorice allsort come to sticky

her daughter, a carnation in high heels,
smelling of a Boots perfumery counter.
They were weather-reported by his father
to the school dance. In the back seat

their hands gazed across the upholstery
at each other like quarantined dogs.
He asked her how she spelled her name
and discovered there should be an i

where he thought there ought to be a y.
They danced shyly, making only shuffling
conversation. At ten forty she mentioned
his tie. 'Do you like it?' he inquired.

'No,' she said. At twelve twenty-five
he returned her to a candlewicked mother,
unrumpled. In the privacy of his room
he tried to magic the evening's facts

by whispering words he wished he'd said.
The group photograph showed him cheesing,
with a long arm around her waist.
And his tie painfully ill with measles.

He sent her the keepsake with much love
and an i not a y. Under the influence
of his spelling, she smiled. Since then
they have kissed and swapped intimacies.

Workout

She watches him pump his flesh: nozzle into his navel,
like a blow-up doll, he swells to latex proportions.

He stretches his physique on medieval racks and performs
the endless repetitive movements of the damned,

while his sweat incontinently dribbles on apparatus.
He lifts millstones with one hand, rubber tubing veins

parcelling his globs of muscle with blue ropes.
She observes his mirror image in designer sportswear

swagger mindlessly to non-stop radio hits and DJ banter.
His musclebound ego flaps arms from the elbow only:

other clubmembers walk precisely the same way.
They recognize each other by this disfigurement.

She sees females, mythic warriors with gladiator arms
and the lips and lashes of angels, winking at her boy.

They push iron until breasts evolve into pectorals,
and thighs become constrictors. After the session,

his mind scorched by sauna and high-protein rivalry,
he emerges in loosefitting chinos, sanctified

with showergel and deodorant. She climbs aboard
his arm and they drive off together into the sunset.

Wordpills

Take these words, they're good for you,
they'll soothe your pain away.
They're coated with a microscopic layer
       of meaning to make them easier to swallow,
so take them twice a day.

Family House

The detached house her father bought reeks
of burning sulphur. White ghosts of steam
hiss from the edges of wall-to-wall carpets.

The dining table trembles on its spindly legs,
the tail of ginger Tom is singed charcoal,
and molten lava glows beneath kitchen tiles.

The garden shed lurches on its green ocean
and the ashen Volvo rocks like a baby's cradle.
Yet her father considers the house a bargain:

while Jove wrestles with the Titans he fiddles
books, balancing investment against interest.
He believes the survey is phoney – no one would

build a house on a magma chamber. He pours
his tea as if he were enjoying eternal life.
Vestigial memories of Krakatoa and Vesuvius

reflect in the kettle: the charred remains
of children embalmed in black crusts of fear;
the upheaval of civilizations; the fountains

of fire that sear the retina. In the workroom
her mother measures the demonic apertures
of wallcracks and prays to Valium for mercy.

A Many-Splendoured Doughnut

The optimist: It's a round pastry,
the pessimist: It's just a hole,
the dualist: Both are quite tasty,
the animist: Thanks to its soul.

The chemist: Carbons and sugars,
the physicist: Atoms and space,
the dentist: Decaying molars,
the evangelist: Edible grace.

The analyst: Oral regressive,
the behaviourist: Hunger response,
the pragmatist: Calories excessive,
the fatalist: Try it but once.

The capitalist: Mouthful of profit,
the marxist: Capitalist greed!
the hedonist: Junk food and scoff it,
the egotist: Just what I need.

The symbolist: Ring of great power,
the cubist: A circular square,
the realist: A thing to devour,
the impressionist: Light, shadow, air!

The idealist: Halo in batter,
the platonist: Great Sugared Roll!
the materialist: What does it matter?
the monist: A part of the whole.

The existentialist: Well-fried in being,
the moralist: Sweet as a sin,
the determinist: Can't help agreeing,
the sophist: Where does it begin?

The Cobra Lighthouse

Six pints of English beer can't flatten him:
his bravado soars above French conversation
like a Spitfire singlehandedly winning a war.
His confidence with girls, intact as a black
porcelain Porsche, glistens between smiling
teeth. 'Here we go, here we go, here we go!'

He backseat drives to the lighthouse in a car
stuffed with reckless English girls and boys.
'Vous voulez monter, monsieur?' Dauntlessly
he slaps uncounted francs into a corroded tin
as his hand brazenly caresses an English bum.
Corkscrewing up the staircase, their tipsy

laughter echoes in the well. Third flight up,
he sobers. His eyes petrify on the cracked
hospital-blue tiles. The rusting metal above
spirals like the bore of a rifle ad infinitum:
he hangs paralysed on his perch as the white
trainers of the girl recede into the heights.

'Here we go, here we go, here we go!' His one
hand clasps the banister, its anaconda curve
supported by see-through railings; the other
panics down the surface of blue tiles, feeling
for normality. *'Vous voulez monter, monsieur?'*
As he touches earth, a man hoists his carefree

child over his shoulders and begins to ascend.
The carful of youths have reached the summit:
they wave down to him from the outside balcony
with hair strewn by sea-breezes. He cranes
his neck to see the girl looking down on him.
Back at campsite, his tent has become a hole

as colossal as a lighthouse. Day after day,
a leper douses himself in the cold Atlantic,
his Porsche melted on a French beach. He sees
no one sunbathing – not even topless chicks.
The lighthouse beams its incessant warning:
painted white at the base, its top half is red

as a bloody finger. Everyone knows he didn't
make it. For him the lighthouse is topless.
He plays endless beach tennis with himself,
bouncing blue tile images against his vertigo:
a lighthouse keeper sliding down the banister
like an impish child; or a harlequined acrobat

flying up the stairwell, then cartwheeling off
the open balcony into a boundless dream-sky.
But he's stuck on the third flight, a chicken
bone in a gullet, which six pints of English
beer will not dislodge. On the seventh day
he returns to the lighthouse alone. The Cobra

rears its pointed head into the venomous blue.
'*Vous voulez monter, monsieur?*' Restricting
his fear with sunglasses, he begins to climb.
Past the third flight, the fourth, the fifth.
The walls narrow like stacked playing cards.
Eighth, ninth – there can't be much farther!

At the tenth, the tube is lit by a sudden red.
Only half-way? His knockknees are shrapnelled
by attacks of dizziness. Next day he reaches
the fifth flight when two coachloads of German
teenagers storm the tower, trooping to the top
with precision and *Deutschtechnik*: his defeat

is their victory. Drenched hours of dinghying
are punctured by the sight of a Cobra's fang.
Windsurfing is blown out by a gust of terror.
Unrelenting sun blisters his pale yellow skin,
but no hydrolizing cream relieves humiliation.
Humans have limits: not everyone can tightrope

or trapeze the Eiffel Tower. Yet even females
and four-year-olds prance daringly to the top!
A day before the holiday terminates, he floats
up through the red artery, holding his breath.
Don't look down! Built in 1905, the supports
and iron bolts are abscessed with corrosion.

Unexpectedly, the flat whiteness of a ceiling –
and the staircase unwinds into a round chamber,
recognized from dreams, where the hooded dread
lies coiled. He tiptoes across a cement hymen
stretched over the well below, while the beast
sleeps. Twelve steps up a steep wooden ladder,

he is born into blue sky. Exulting seagulls
squawk acclamations as he circles the balcony,
wings flapping to faceless spectators beneath.
His last night is spent intimately with mates,
enjoying six pints of quenching English beer
and the consolations of a frothy English girl.

The lone Spitfire has returned – damaged, but
heroic. 'Here we go, here we go, here we go!'

My Party

The intrepid gang of five hunt the pavements
for my house, camouflaged as it is between

many houses. They stash cider handgrenades
on the garage roof under my father's eyes

before ringing the doorbell. Potplants curl
their roots in tight shoes, refusing to dance.

My parents huddle in their bedroom, peeping
through curtains but pretending unconcern.

The party starts with sofa-cushion football,
kung fu with the peanut-bowl, spin the bottle

with dumb-giggly forfeits, and spray painting
the ceiling with Pepsi. As the cider explodes,

the intrepids, moved by cortexripping rhythms,
try to practise their sumo dancing on females.

Potplants fold their aching leaves. A war
of marshmallows and Maltesers is followed

by a crisp potato hurricane leaving the dead
and dying chocolates to bleed sog and gunge

on a mock Axminster battlefield. A gaggle
of girls in black skirts with sham zips

incite their warriors by flaunting breasts
and ululating from the skirting boards.

The wild things rumpus. Boys with beaks
and headfeathers howl and bellow and bark,

duelling for supremacy with antlers clashing.
Midnight is chimed by the smashing of windows

and my parents swiftly abandon their vigil.
They dustpan the debris and tend the wounded.

'Parents showing up at a party! Yuuuugh!'
The gang of five in their wolf-suits steal out

into the night jungle where the slow music
cannot harm them. Lingering couples sway

on the dancefloor, trailing in spilled cider.
Potplants dance together. I am a year older.

The River

Where have I been
    and where am I going?
Am I the river
    or am I the flowing?

What have I done
    and who has been doing?
Am I the actor
    or critic reviewing?

What have I touched
    and who has been feeling?
Am I the owner
    or thief caught stealing?

What have I seen
    and what has been showing?
Am I the light
    or the eye all-knowing?

What have I said
    and who has been hearing?
Am I the helper
    or one who needs caring?

What have I lost
    and who has been finding?
Am I the forgetting
    or am I the reminding?

Who have I hurt
    and who has been crying?
Am I the living
    or am I the dying?